How to use this book

Follow the advice, in italics, given for you on each page.
Support the children as they read the text that is shaded in cream.
***Praise** the children at every step!*

Detailed guidance is provided in the Read Write Inc. Phonics Handbook

9 reading activities

Children:
Practise reading the speed sounds.
Read the green, red and challenge words for the story.
Listen as you read the introduction.
Discuss the vocabulary check with you.
Read the story.
Re-read the story and discuss the 'questions to talk about'.
Read the story with fluency and expression.
Answer the questions to 'read and answer'.
Practise reading the speed words.

Speed sounds

Consonants *Say the pure sounds (do not add 'uh').*

f ff	l ll	m mm	n nn **kn**	r rr	s ss	v ve	z zz	sh	th	ng nk

b bb	c k ck	d dd	g gg	h	j	p pp	qu	t tt	w **wh**	x	y	ch tch

Vowels *Say the sounds in and out of order.*

at	hen head	in	on	up	day	see happy	high find	blow no

zoo	look	car	for door snore	fair	whirl	shout	boy spoil

*Each box contains **one sound** but sometimes more than one grapheme. Focus graphemes are **circled**.*

Green words

Read in Fred Talk (pure sounds).

lunch look may door

keep meet street see been bleep sheep green three

need knee sheet

Read in syllables.

in\`sect	→	insect	tedd\`y	→	teddy
sec\`ond	→	second	fif\`teen	→	fifteen
six\`teen	→	sixteen	sett\`ee	→	settee
yipp\`ee	→	yippee	a\`sleep	→	asleep

Read the root word first and then with the ending.

dish	→	dishes	feel	→	feeling
wheel	→	wheels	feed	→	feeding

Red words

want all my one we to do you
I'm I've

Challenge words

almost baby both every sister wash pretend
guess

Do we have to keep it?

Introduction

Do you have any brothers or sisters?
How do you feel about them? Dan Reed has a new baby in his family and he's not sure how he feels about it. The baby needs lots of attention from everybody, needs feeding all the time and even wees on his trousers!

He says he doesn't like the baby but do you think he really means that?

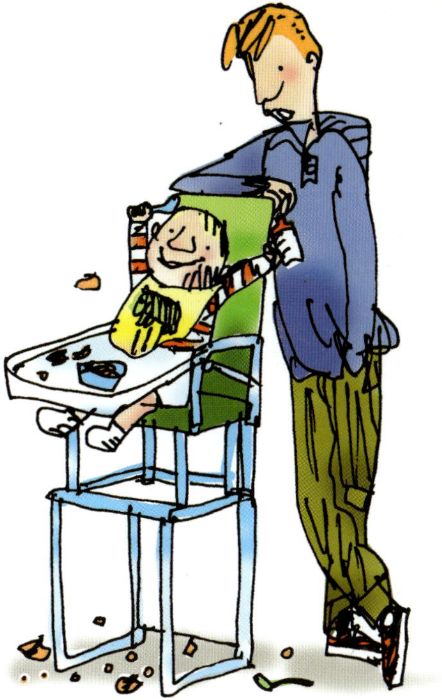

Story written by Gill Munton
Illustrated by Tim Archbold

Vocabulary check

Discuss the meaning (as used in the story) after the children have read each word.

	definition:	sentence/phrase:
stick insect	*an insect that you can keep as a pet*	*I wanted a stick insect.*
settee	*sofa*	*Mum sits on the settee.*
eel	*an underwater snake like animal*	*It's not a baby at all - it's an eel!*
dumps	*drops down, puts*	*Then Mum dumps the baby on my knee.*
combats	*trousers*	*It wees on my best combats!*
creep	*goody goody*	*My sister Sheena is just a creep.*

Punctuation to note in this story:

1. Capital letters to start sentences and full stop to end sentences

2. Capital letters for names

3. Exclamation marks to show anger, shock and surprise

4. 'Wait and see' dots...

Do we have to keep it?

I'm Dan Reed.

I'm almost ten, and I live at

fifteen, Fleetwood Street.

And I've got ... *a baby!*

Well, Mum and Dad have.

And I'm not feeling very happy.

I did tell Mum that I wanted a stick insect,

but no, she went and got a baby.

And no, it cannot go back to the shop!

This baby! It looks very funny.

You want to see it!

Mum sits on the settee,

and sticks the baby on her knee.

It digs its heels into her legs,

and then it kicks with both feet

and twists its body.

It's not a baby at all – it's an eel!

Then the baby needs feeding.

It seems to need feeding every three seconds,

it's so greedy.

Bits of mashed up beef and carrot,

yuk, and milk, milk, milk.

Oh, yes, and it's got this silly bib

with a green sheep on it!

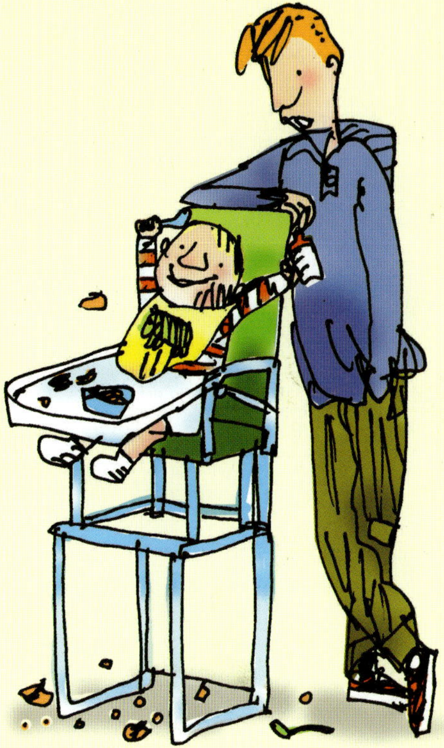

Then Mum dumps the baby on my knee,

so she can wash up the lunch dishes.

The next thing is, it's sick on the sheep bib,

or it wees on my best combats!

I ask Mum, do we have to keep it?

My sister Sheena (she's sixteen)

is just a creep. She gives the baby a

big sloppy kiss, *then* mops it up with

a flannel, and puts it in its buggy.

We set off along Fleetwood Street.
Sheena wheels the buggy, and I pretend
I'm not with them.

If we meet Val from next door,
she greets us with,
"Oh! He's just sooooo sweet!"
No one tells me I'm sweet.
(Not that I want them to.)

When we get back, it's six o'clock and the baby has to go to bed. Mum sticks it in its cot - and sings to it!

It's got a pink teddy that bleeps if you press its tummy.

When it's asleep, at last, we have a bit of a rest from it.

Then it's "Eeeeeeeee! Wheeeeeeee!" and guess what - it's been sick on the sheets.

Yippee! I'm going out for a meal with Dad today.

Just him and me. No baby ...

But I may get the baby a new toy, or a silly hat.

I've got a funny feeling that I'll miss him, just a teeny-weeny bit.

Questions to talk about

Re-read the page. Read the question to the children. Tell them whether it is a **FIND IT** *question or* **PROVE IT** *question.*

FIND IT

- ✓ *Turn to the page*
- ✓ *Read the question*
- ✓ *Find the answer*

PROVE IT

- ✓ *Turn to the page*
- ✓ *Read the question*
- ✓ *Find your evidence*
- ✓ *Explain why*

Page 9:	PROVE IT	*What is Dan upset about?*
Page 10:	PROVE IT	*Why does Dan call the baby 'it' and not by its name?*
Page 11:	FIND IT	*What does the baby eat?*
Page 12:	PROVE IT	*How does Dan feel when he has to hold the baby? Why?*
Page 13:	PROVE IT	*How does Dan feel when people make a fuss of the baby?*
Page 14:	PROVE IT	*How does Mum get the baby to sleep?*
Page 15:	PROVE IT	*Why do you think Dan is so excited about going out?* *What do you think Dan really feels about the baby?*

Questions to read and answer

(Children complete without your help.)

1. What number is Dan's house in Fleetwood Street?
   Dan Reed lives at number **ten / six / fifteen** Fleetwood Street.

2. What sort of pet did Dan want?
   Dan wanted **a puppy / a kitten / a stick insect.**

3. What food did the baby like?
   The baby liked **ham and eggs / mashed up beef and carrots / bread and jam.**

4. What animal is on the baby's bib?
   The baby has a bib with **a green sheep / a pink pig / a red hen** on it.

5. Who does Dan go out for a meal with?
   Dan goes out with **the baby / his dad / his sister.**

Speed words

Children practise reading the words across the rows, down the columns and in and out of order clearly and quickly.

sings	dishes	today	body	tummy
stick	green	need	three	feeling
sheets	sixteen	do	we	I've
sheep	were	wanted	creep	into